Akabish's First Christmas

Dan Bradford

"Akabish's First Christmas," by Dan Bradford. ISBN 978-1-60264-891-3

Published 2011 by Virtualbookworm.com Publishing Inc., P.O. Box 9949, College Station, TX 77842, US.©2011, Dan Bradford. All rights reserved. No part of this publication may be reproduced, stored in a retrieval system, or transmitted in any form or by any means, electronic, mechanical, recording or otherwise, without the prior written permission of Dan Bradford.

Manufactured in the United States of America.

I would like to tell you a story about a lady by the name of Akabish. You may think it's an odd name, but it was her mother's name and her mother's mother's as far back as she could understand. You see, "Akabish" is the Hebrew name meaning "swift weaver." It also means "spider." Our lady was a spider that lived in a manger not far from a large human city. From her perch high up in the rafters of the manger, she could see many humans coming and going on the road that led from the city. She often wondered how so many humans could live in such a small space! She was happy that she had her own place to live and many places to spin her webs.

4

The manger that was her home was owned by a herdsman and his family. She could see his home from her web. They would come to the manger to feed the animals every day and night. He would take his herd of sheep out away from the manger in the morning and bring them back at night. She often wondered where they went and what they did out of sight of the manger.

5

Akabish had spun many webs in the manger. There was one that she was most proud of. It spanned across what seemed to her to be a very large hole high up on the side wall of the manger. It was a place where she could catch the large black flies that flew in the manger to torment the animals that lived and ate there. There was only one problem with this perfect place. The bird which made its nest on the other side of the manger would forget the web was there and fly in through the opening. Each time she did, she would rip a big hole in the web that would have to be repaired. Every time it happened, the bird would chirp her apology. It seemed to happen most often right after the bird's eggs hatched and her young were calling to her for food. Akabish thought that her own young would never be so demanding. They would have to get their own food as soon as they had hatched.

During this year, she had seen many of the animals that lived in the manger give birth. Akabish had seen the cow that the humans milked each morning give birth to a calf in the spring. She remembered how the mother cow had licked and nudged the calf to encourage it to stand soon after it was born. She watched as the calf took its first drink of its mother's milk. Again, Akabish thought that it was very inconvenient to have the young new-born so dependent on its mother for food, but the mother cow didn't seem to mind.

7

Later that spring, the sheep began to have their young in the same manner. They would be born and then they would be encouraged by their mothers to stand. She could see that the mothers took very good care of their babies. She watched each one being born and then struggle to its feet. Each one, in turn, would wobble and stumble at first. Within just a short time, they were running and playing with each other. The sight was most entertaining.

As the summer passed, Akabish watched the young that had been born in the spring grow to nearly adult size. She saw how they became part of the herd and that made the entire family better because they were there. She could see how the mothers would continue to look out for their young until they had grown enough to take care of themselves. She saw the young humans come out of the house to help with the chores. She thought that they were either small human adults or that they didn't grow as fast as the other creatures she watched. She had never seen a human being born.

9

Now that summer had passed and the late fall had turned cold, Akabish was preparing for the winter that was soon to be upon them. She was busy spinning a nest where her young would be born in the spring. Just then, the bird flew into the manger through the hole where Akabish had spun her web. The bird chirped an apology as she flew to her perch in the rafters of the manger. It was getting near dark and many of the animals were coming in for their evening feeding and to settle in for the night.

10

Akabish was feeling especially good today even though she couldn't figure out why. She didn't mind having to repair the web the bird had torn. As she began to repair it, she thought of new ways to make it even better. She took extra time to spin a very special web. It took her nearly an hour before she put the last strands in place. It was a fine web with many new patterns. She had never woven a web like that before and she felt quite proud of it as she made her way up to her evening perch to admire her work.

11

As she sat watching the animals eating and the humans coming and going taking care of their chores, she could see a very bright star appear in the East. "That is strange," she thought. She had never seen that star before. It was very bright. The humans noticed it too. They stood, looking up at it and talking to each other about it as they walked back to their house.

12

Not long after the humans had left the manger, they came back. They had a human man and woman with them whom she had never seen before. The young woman seemed to be uncomfortable. The herdsman spread out some fresh straw in the manger and put down a blanket for the young woman. It all seemed very strange for Akabish. She watched intently as the woman lay down on the blanket. Soon, the herdsman's wife came out with the wife of the herdsman's son.

13

Akabish watched every move as the two older women pushed the men out of the manger and placed blankets over the young lady resting there. The events were strange to Akabish until it became very clear to her. The young lady on the blanket was going to give birth! Akabish moved to a better place from which to watch. She had never seen a human being born and she didn't want to miss out on any of it.

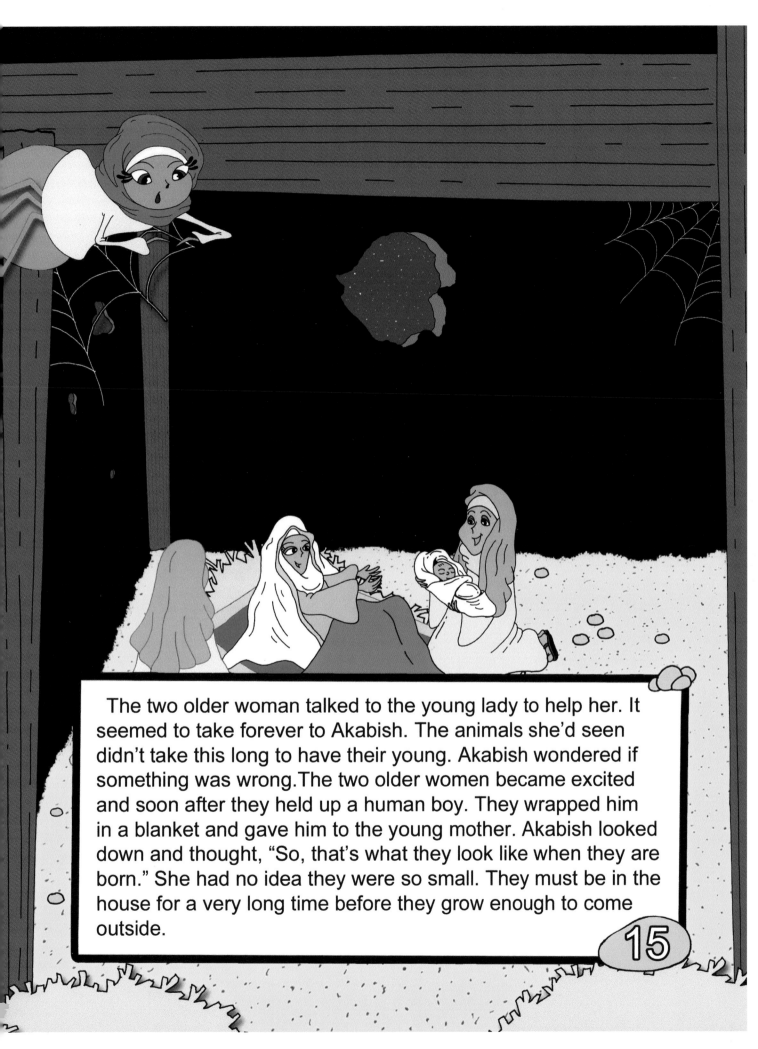

The two older woman talked to the young lady to help her. It seemed to take forever to Akabish. The animals she'd seen didn't take this long to have their young. Akabish wondered if something was wrong. The two older women became excited and soon after they held up a human boy. They wrapped him in a blanket and gave him to the young mother. Akabish looked down and thought, "So, that's what they look like when they are born." She had no idea they were so small. They must be in the house for a very long time before they grow enough to come outside.

15

The young mother took her baby and held him close to her. Akabish could not see what was happening then, but she knew from watching the other animals that the baby must be feeding. She knew that all animals were born hungry. And, it seemed that this human baby was no different. She thought how wonderful it was to be there when this baby was born.

16

The bright star in the sky was shining down and it seemed to be spreading its light on the manger. Akabish could see that there were many humans coming from different directions. They all seemed to be coming to the manger. She watched as they gathered around the shelter and knelt. She had never seen this before. No other birth had ever received this kind of attention. She thought that this child must be very special to have all of these humans coming to be here with him and his mother.

17

One at a time, the humans who had gathered brought gifts of all types and laid them at the feet of the new mother and her son. Three men who Akabish did not recognize rode up on camels. She had seen most of the herdsmen and their families before as they had come and gone with their flocks. These three men on camels had never been here before. She had never seen humans in clothes like that. The colors were so bright and they seemed to sparkle. "They must be very important men," she thought.

18

The three men slid off their camels and walked to the manger. They knelt and placed gifts at the feet of the mother and her son. The gifts seemed to be as important as the men giving them. Akabish was puzzled by all this. She had never seen the birth of a human before, but this could not be what happened all the time. This must be a very special event for the humans. She watched as the three men walked back to the herdsmen and knelt.

19

Both a feeling of joy and sadness crept over Akabish. It was wonderful to be here for such an event, but she didn't have anything to give the mother and her baby. The thought made her very sad. How could she give this very important baby and his mother a gift? All she knew how to do was to spin webs. It didn't seem that the young mother and her son needed a web.

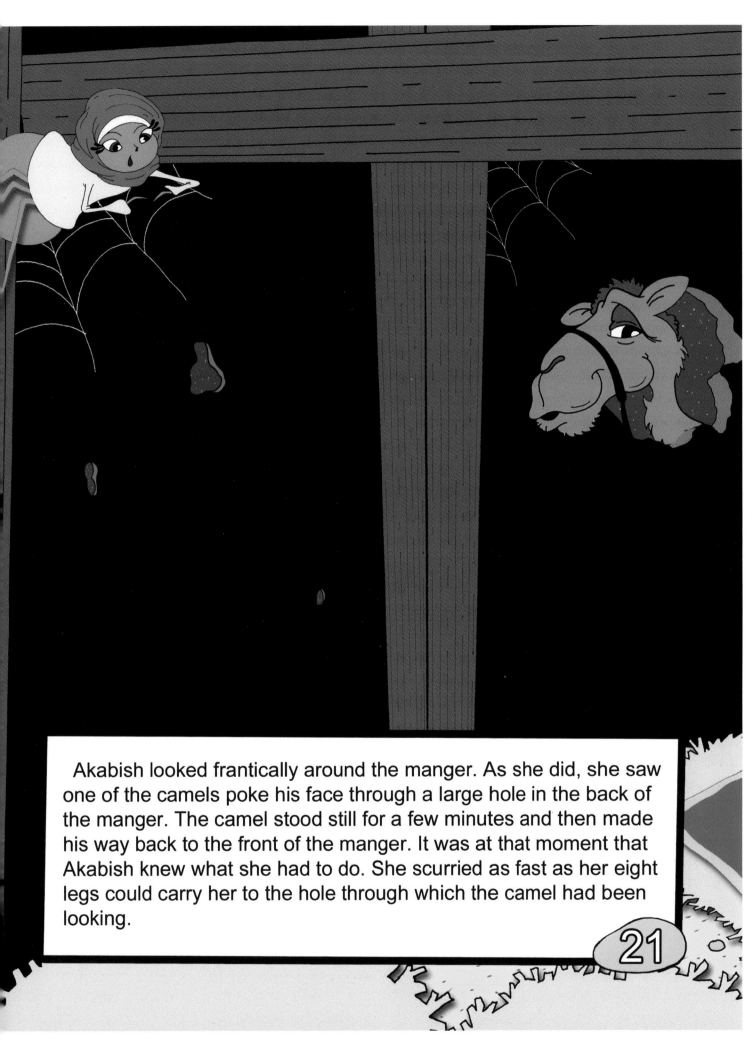

Akabish looked frantically around the manger. As she did, she saw one of the camels poke his face through a large hole in the back of the manger. The camel stood still for a few minutes and then made his way back to the front of the manger. It was at that moment that Akabish knew what she had to do. She scurried as fast as her eight legs could carry her to the hole through which the camel had been looking.

21

She began to spin a web. She darted back and forth in the opening. It was very large and she had never tried to fill a space this big before. Now she went up and down and from side to side again. She had to hurry. She was running out of time and if she didn't finish soon, her gift would never be noticed and all of this would have been done for nothing. Her movements became faster and faster as she rushed to fill the opening.

22

Nearly two hours had passed and she was very tired. She couldn't stop now. It was nearly finished and her time was almost up. There... she had the final parts of her web in place and just in time. She was very tired but pleased as she made her way back up to her perch high in the rafters of the manger.

23

As she reached her home, she turned to see what her efforts had created. The first rays of light from the bright star were streaming through the opening in the wall of the manger. As the light passed through the web, it was transformed into the most beautiful rainbow of colors and patterns. The wonderful colored light washed over the young mother and her son. It painted them in its beauty. The baby looked up at where Akabish was perched and smiled. The young mother turned her head to see where the light was coming from. She also smiled in appreciation for the gift that Akabish had created. The light was brighter now as it made circles of light over the heads of the mother and her son. The web seemed to shimmer for the longest time!

24

Akabish was pleased to see that her gift had been seen by the mother and her son. She settled back into her home and felt warmed by the events. It was a wonderful night, one that she would never forget.

25

Dan Bradford is the father of three daughters and the grandfather to six boys and three girls. The story of Akabish's First Christmas was originally written to be read to his family on Christmas Eve. Mr. Bradford comes from a strong and loving family background. He will tell his family "Birthdays and Anniversaries are fine but it's Christmas when I can really show all of you how much I love you by giving you not only presents but a part of myself." That is why he wrote this story. Now he would like to share it with all of you. A special gift from his family to yours.

Saydee Lanes entered a contest that Mr. Bradford created to find a talented young artist to illustrate his books. Ms. Lanes was selected out of several candidates from the four local high schools. She is an accomplished artist with several awards for her work. She looks forward to continuing her work as founder of "Loop Bear Illustrations" after graduation.